H̶ ̶ ̶-Y

to Lauren

Best Wishes

Nigel Planer

First published in 1996 by Sapling,
an imprint of Boxtree Ltd, Broadwall House,
21 Broadwall, London SE1 9PL
Copyright © Geoffrey Planer, 1996

10 9 8 7 6 5 4 3 2 1

Reproduction by SX Composing DTP
Printed and bound in Great Britain by Cambus Litho Ltd.

ISBN: 0 7522 2310 0

A CIP catalogue entry for this book
is available from the British Library.

MOUSE TALES

Little Hysteria's
Extra Messy Spell

Geoffrey Planer

⏺ sapling

For Thea
(who isn't at all)

'I want a glass of water.'
'You're supposed to be asleep,'
said Mrs Tail from the doorway.
'Well I didn't have a story.'
'Get back into bed and I'll get one.'
'A story?'
'A glass of water,' said Mrs Tail firmly.
'Could I have a glass of story instead?'
'Very funny Louisa. Now into bed.'
'But I didn't have a story.'
'Well, it's too late and I'm certainly not
reading you one now,' said Mrs Tail,
as she sat down on the bed
and started to read one.

Another Night,
Another Mouse,
Another Tale . . .

Little Hysteria's
Extra Messy Spell

Once upon a time there lived a
Fairy Godmother called Mrs Wysteria.
She lived in a cottage in an enchanted
wood with her Fairy Goddaughter
called Little Hysteria.

On Mondays, Wednesdays and Fridays, Mrs Wysteria was on Wish Duty. She would usually get a phone call from someone on Earth who really, really, really needed a wish to come true.

Then she would pick up her handbag,
take her wand down from the shelf,
get on her golden bicycle and
pedal off into the clouds.

On Tuesdays
and Thursdays
(and, of course,
Saturdays
and Sundays
and holidays),
she would
stay home
with Little
Hysteria.

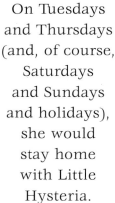

On the days when Mrs Wysteria had to go out to work, Mrs Mac from across the road would fly in to baby-sit.

Mrs Mac was nice, but she didn't play quite the right sort of games. In fact, the only thing that Little Hysteria really, really, really wished for was someone with whom to play those right sort of games.

But Mrs Wysteria was always busy with
Away Wishes and never seemed to
get around to Home Wishes.

Little Hysteria was not actually that Little.
She was quite able to look after herself
and things, Thank You Very Much, and
she knew quite a lot about loads of things,
and she could even do quite a few spells
and things, and she did not really
need baby-sitting and things at all,
Thank You Very Much.

Now, of course, Little Hysteria had promised her mother that she would never do anything silly in the house while her mother was away and Mrs Mac was there. Especially not if ...

Mrs Mac were ever to fall asleep ... reading the newspaper. And so ...

... one Monday evening at half past six Mrs Wysteria came back home, tired out after a good day's good-doing. She opened the door to the cottage, looking forward to a nice cup of tea and a chocolate cookie,

and then, to her surprise,

she found a
very large
pink toad
asleep on
the sofa.

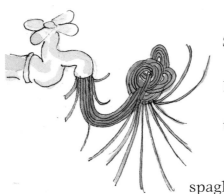

She went into
the kitchen,
picked up the
kettle and
turned on the
tap. Instead
of water, blue
spaghetti shot out.

She opened
the fridge –
in it were
twenty-four
blackbirds
singing.

She opened
the biscuit
tin – sitting
inside was a
big green spider
in a hat.

'Hysteria ...'
she shouted.
'Come here!
AT ONCE!'

Hysteria came
out from the
cupboard,
where she
had been
hiding.

'Who did this?' Mrs Wysteria asked
pointing to a chair stuck to the ceiling.
'Must have been the Other Hysteria,'
said Hysteria, pretending not
to know anything.

'And who did this?' Mrs Wysteria asked, pointing to the blue giraffe in the washing machine.

'Must have been that Other Hysteria,' said Hysteria.

'And who turned the telly into jelly?
And the clock into chocolate?
And the coffee into toffee?
And the ...'

'Must've been the Other Hysteria.'
'And the frying pan into fish-cakes?'

At that moment there was a
thundering noise down the
stairs and a small dragon
ran excitedly into the
room. It snorted out
fiery little sparks
from its nose
as it came up
to lick Mrs Wysteria's hand.

Then it lay down on
its back for a
tickle, waggling
its legs in the
air. It played
just the right
sort of games.

'And I suppose that Other Hysteria magicked him out of a bottle of shampoo?' said Mrs Wysteria. 'Toothpaste actually,' said Hysteria. 'Oh can't we keep him? Please, please, pretty please?' she went on in her Little Voice, rubbing the back of her leg with her shoe.

Mrs Wysteria looked stern
and thought for a bit.
'All right, if that's what you
really wish for,' she said.
Hysteria nodded her head very fast.
'But you must make a spell that clears up
all the mess you've made this instant ...

AND ...

... make a spell that makes that Other
Hysteria disappear this instant ...

AND ...

... make another spell that turns poor Mrs Mac back from being a big pink toad ...

... THIS INSTANT!'

Hysteria stopped nodding her head. They both looked at the big pink toad, which was still lying fast asleep on the sofa, snoring, with the newspaper lying beside it.

'Goodness me,' said Mrs Tail,
looking at the glass of water.
'Whatever is that in there, Lou?'
'What?' asked Louisa wide-eyed.
'There it is again.'
'What? WHERE?' said Louisa, sitting
straight up in bed, looking worried.
'In the glass of water. There it goes again.
It's a big pink toad,' said Mrs Tail,
peering into the glass.
Louisa looked closely. 'I can't see it,' she said.
'No – it's just vanished. Must be a magic one,'
said Mrs Tail.
'I don't believe you. You're teasing,' said Louisa.
'Nighty-night, Lou.'
'Night-night,' said Lou, looking at
the glass of water again, just in case.

Small Tales,
Tall Tales,
Bedtime -
for All Tails